The wood across the road from us is not that big at all.
In fact compared to other woods it's actually quite small.

Be sure to bring your friends along and never stray apart,
as you shouldn't enter on your own, or go there when it's dark.

In the middle of the wood there stands a huge oak tree,

it stands above the rest more than 100 of you or me.

At the base of its trunk there looms a large dark hole,
but this deep pit was not dug by any fox or mole.

For years we've heard the stories
of things that go bump in the dark.
Things they say are special to our leafy landmark.

We've never thought that much of them, just stories to be told.

But carry on reading…

…our adventure is about to unfold.

A cottage in the countryside is where we should begin,
where a family of young adventurers sleep snuggly within.
One night they heard a noise of
something quite peculiar,

jumping from their beds,
they ran to hold each other.

Crash
Thump
Wallop!

It sounds again,
and then once more...
but silence follows after.

Then **suddenly,** from rooms
downstairs they hear some cheerful laughter.

"PJ's check…

Slippers check…"

a flashlight grabbed in hand…

They move downstairs at tip-toe speed,
with each one hand-in-hand.

Giggle Giggle
Ha Ha Ha

"There's nothing here. No wait… what's that? It's coming from outside",

they crept to the window,
to see what they had spied.

"A cat?", said one,

another shouts "FOX?",

but none of these creatures were there.

"Hang on a minute, is that…
…could it be?

MUSHROOMS STEALING OUR COOKWARE?"

As plain as day (although it was night), the family stood in wonder, as 3 little mushrooms 2 feet high stood with their bag of plunder. They shuffled across the flower beds, over the fence, then the road, through the gate and into the woods, surrounded by a strange green glow.

"Is this all a dream? It cannot be real!
Are the stories actually true?"

"We need to find out, we need to go now,
let's follow this motley crew".

They ran upstairs and into their rooms,
they put on their clothes with haste.

Into the night, across to the wood, but the
creatures had vanished without trace!

"Onward ho",
they started to search, but "nothing" they could find.

Even with the flashlight,
they thought they'd all gone blind.

Suddenly, from up ahead, a chuckling laugh was heard.
They poked a bush, out came a cry, it's hiding place disturbed.

With dazzled eyes and throbbing chests, tears rolling down their cheeks, the fugitives fell to the ground and one began to speak.

"Don't hurt us, please, we mean no harm. It's not us you should fear.

Come quick, let's move to somewhere safe, as dangers closing near"

The moon shone down from above, revealing strange new places.
The winds began to howl and moan, waking weird new faces.

In the trees above their heads and deep beneath the ground,
in tunnels winding through the earth...
strange creatures could be found.

They raced through the undergrowth, splashing through the mud.
Behind the fleeing troop they heard a

Thud, Thud, Thud.

A little mushroom shouted back
"We're almost there...
through here"

The family followed as fast as they could,
their hearts filling with fear.

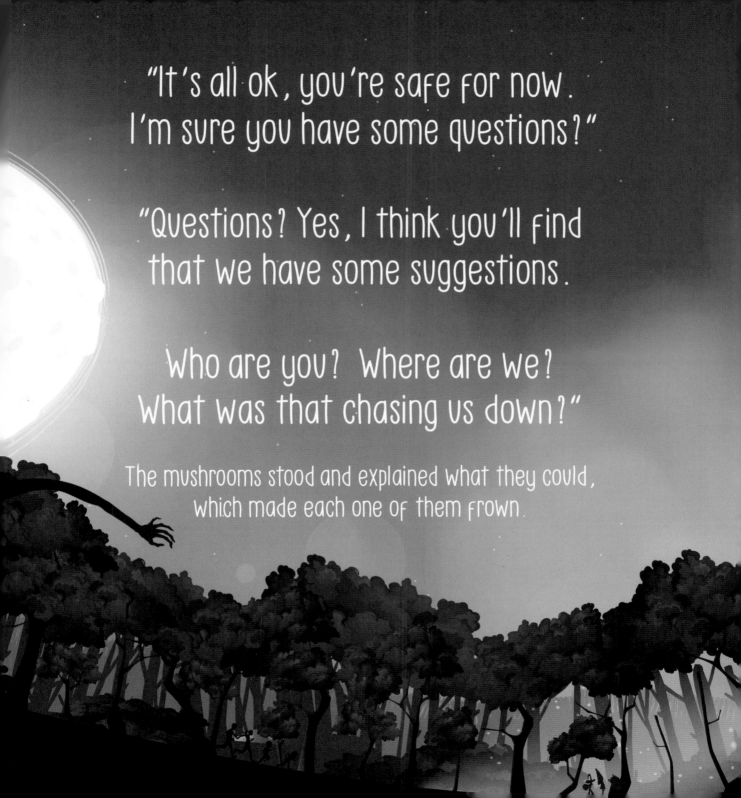

"It's all ok, you're safe for now.
I'm sure you have some questions?"

"Questions? Yes, I think you'll find
that we have some suggestions.

Who are you? Where are we?
What was that chasing us down?"

The mushrooms stood and explained what they could,
which made each one of them frown.

"We are the Shroombooms, and we mean you no harm, we're sorry to have caused you any alarm"

"This is our home,
safe and hidden away and for now at least,
we'd ask you to stay"

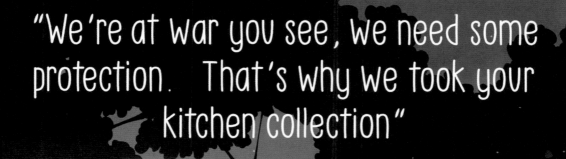

"We're at war you see, we need some protection.   That's why we took your kitchen collection"

"The knives and the forks, the pots and the pans, they make awesome protection from our enemy clans"

"The Stinklers,
made from mud and stone,
smell really bad,
and voice a terrible groan.

They're sticky and cruel
and oozing with pus...

For years, they've been collecting us!

A Shroomboom stepped forward and lifted their cap,
revealing what was below.
A stone that sparkled and shone in the night,
surrounded by a mysterious glow.

"These are the seeds of this woodland
retreat, without them it wouldn't be here.
They help the plants grow, the animals too,
without them we'd all disappear"

"The Stinklers want them for themselves,
so they can control this land,
So let's call on our friends, that live in this
wood to help us in our stand.

I'm sure with your help,
along with theirs too,
we can form a mighty army.
To help defeat our enemies
and end this perilous journey"

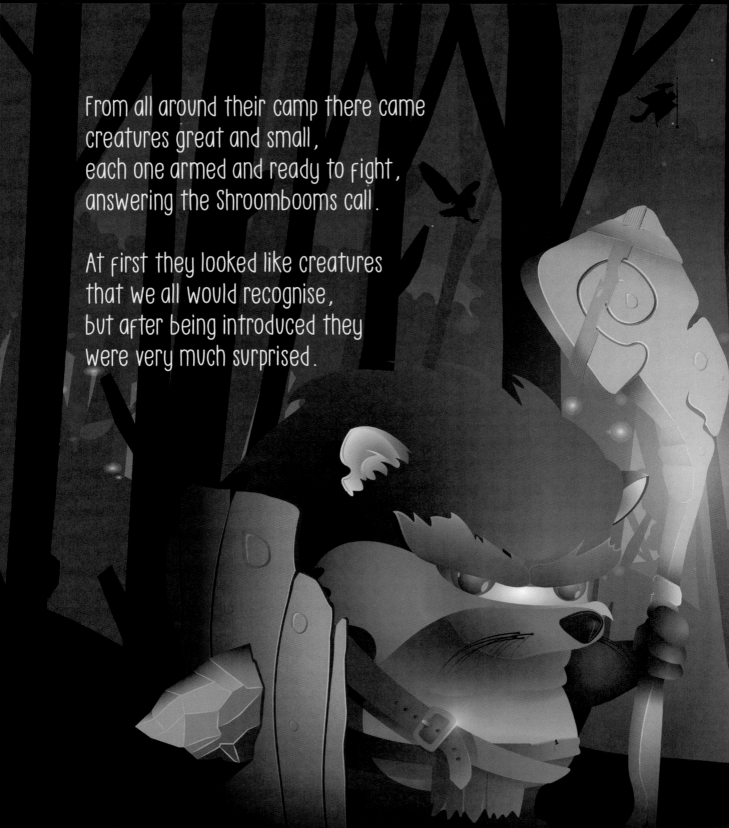

From all around their camp there came
creatures great and small,
each one armed and ready to fight,
answering the Shroombooms call.

At first they looked like creatures
that we all would recognise,
but after being introduced they
were very much surprised.

The Hedg-e-mogs were first to stand,
ready and waiting in line,

Each protected by a coat with more than 5000 spines.

"Our legs are tiny,
but don't dismay
we don't intend to crawl.

We'll roll this enemy out
of this wood, with an
attack of spikey balls"

The **Nibble-chippers** glided down from the trees,
their arms stretched out wide.
In the branches high above is where they liked to hide.

"We may not look that fierce with this
fluffy tail in our butts,
but we're ready and waiting to fight …
as long as you give us some nuts"

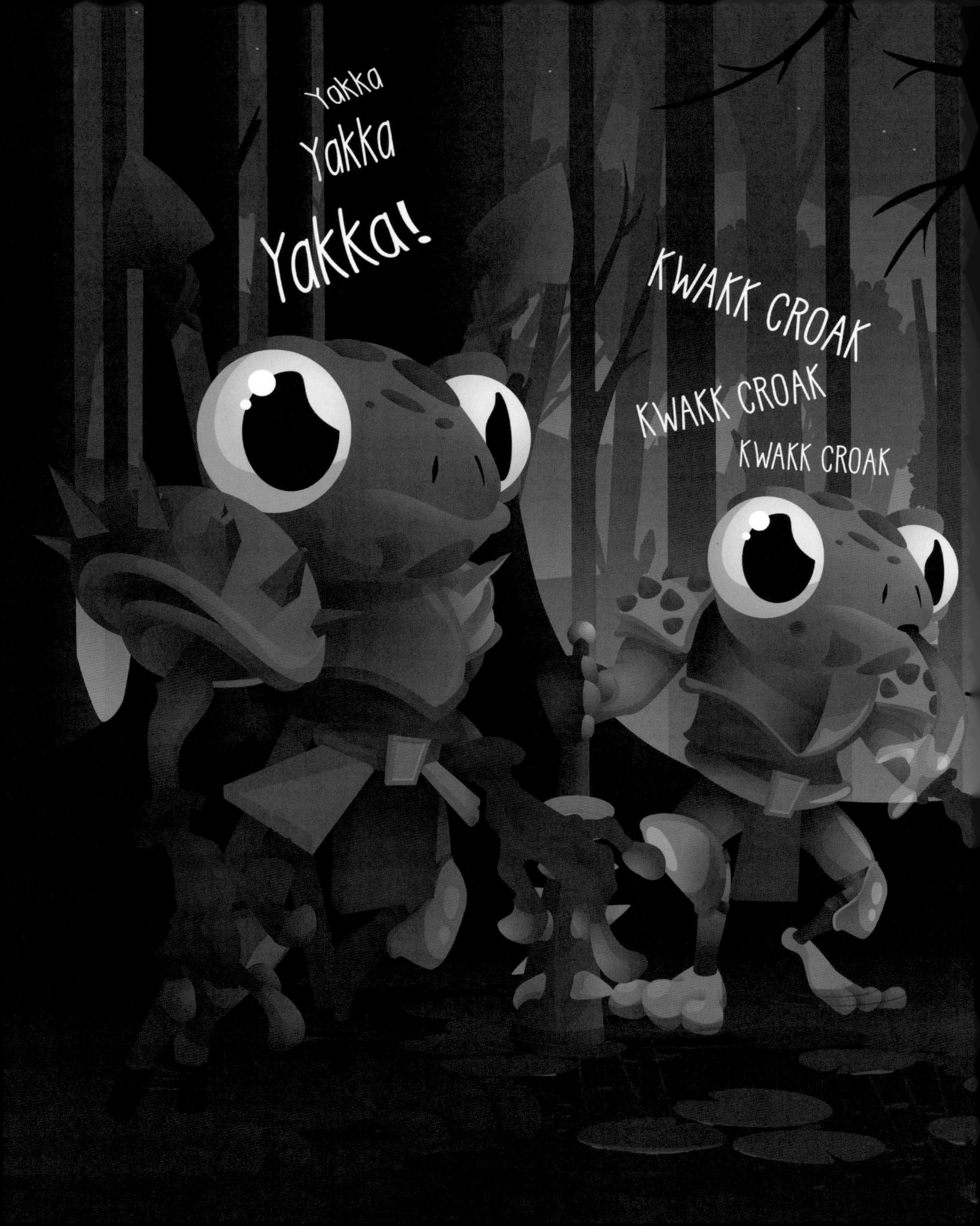
Yakka
Yakka
Yakka!
KWAKK CROAK
KWAKK CROAK
KWAKK CROAK

Bounding in, to join the team
the Hop-a-lots leaped to the ground.
Everyone covered their ears
from their horrid croaking sound.

RIBBIT - RIBBIT

"We'll jump on top of the enemy, and
squash them beneath our feet,
then we can all celebrate and
this quest will be complete"

The wise old **Hootlings** stood silent,
their eyes as wide as could be.
Their heads turning full circle,
watching everything they could see.

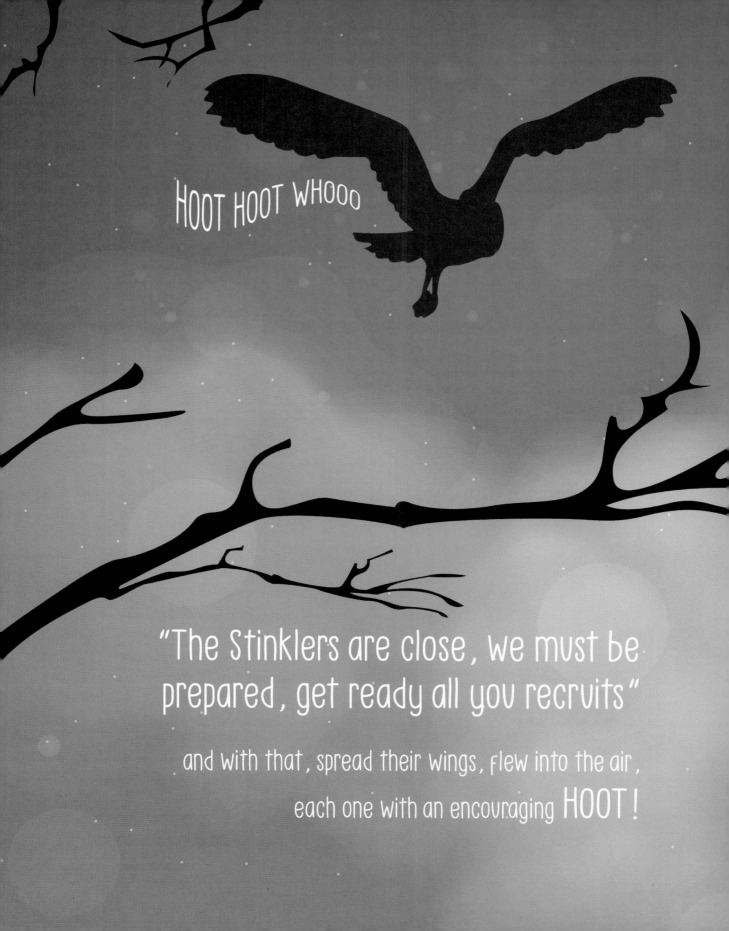

HOOT HOOT WHOOO

"The Stinklers are close, we must be prepared, get ready all you recruits"

and with that, spread their wings, flew into the air,
each one with an encouraging HOOT !

"So what's the plan? We can't beat them with force. I thought you all tried that before"

"Ah yes, we did and it didn't go well, but back then we didn't have you four.

A family's love is stronger than what we could do alone, & together we will have the power to protect our precious gemstones"

The family smiled and gave a hug
to each and every member,
of their new found friends, found at night,
a night they'd surely remember.

Standing tall and ready for battle,
they headed out into the woods,
the plan, so simple, "to work together"
was one they all understood.

The silence of the misty wood made every whisper deafening.
The inky blackness of the night made everything look
threatening. Through the shadows came a stench, a rumble and

a roar, as the Stinklers rose up from their pit,

it was an all-out-war.

The **Nibble-chippers** first attacked, dropping from the trees, while the **Hop-a-lots** lept to the skies bringing **Stinklers** to their knees. The **Hedg-e-mogs** rolled in fast and spikes flew through the air, with everyone attacking they were defeating this nightmare.

It seemed as if the war was won, the Stinklers faced defeat, but none of our heroes prepared for what they would now meet. The last few Stinklers turned and held each other by the hand, they merged into a

GIANT

ready for one last stand.

Slowly rising to its feet, the giant snarled and wailed. Our friends despaired

"All hope is gone, our plan has surely failed"

The family, dazed by what they saw, quickly changed the tone,

"Shroombooms…
quickly, remove your hats,
use the power of your
gemstones"

The **Shroombooms** lifted up their caps,
and bent their heads down low.
Each crystal shone a stream of light,
the wood filled with the glow.
The creatures and the family too,
gathered round while chanting,

"Take this wicked creature down,
hit them with your lightning"

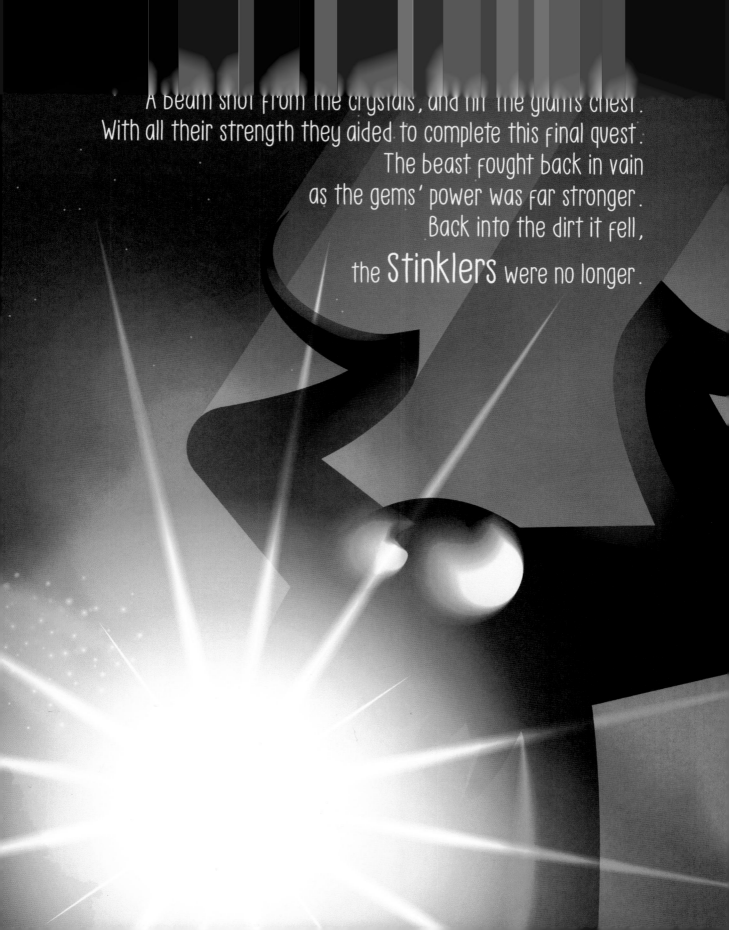

A beam shot from the crystals, and hit the giants chest.
With all their strength they aided to complete this final quest.
The beast fought back in vain
as the gems' power was far stronger.
Back into the dirt it fell,
the Stinklers were no longer.

A cry of joy was sounded from each corner of the land,
with each creature working together,
everything went as planned.

They gathered back to celebrate with happiness and cheer,
and partied until morning time without an ounce of fear.

At dawn the creatures gathered round
to thank their new found friends.

"You helped us bring our enemy
and this war to an end.
We haven't much to offer you,
we can give only this"

as a Shroomboom placed around
their necks, a gemstone necklace.

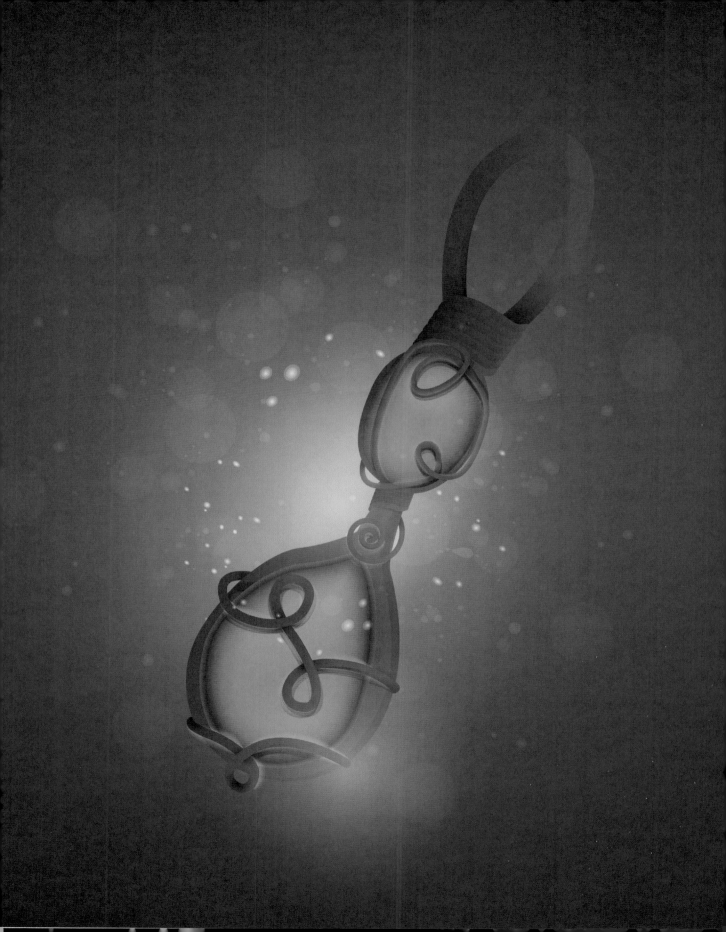

"These will keep you safe and remind you of your time here"

Then one by one, the creatures turned
and magically disappeared.

With heads deep in thought, our family started walking home,
this time knowing that they were not walking alone.

So the next time you're
thinking of taking a walk...
climbing up trees or jumping off rocks.

Listen to my story and try to be good...
as you never know what's hiding
in your local wood.

Printed in Great Britain
by Amazon